# WHEN MOLLY WAS IN THE HOSPITAL

# WHEN MOLLY
# WAS IN THE HOSPITAL

A Book for Brothers and Sisters
of Hospitalized Children

DEBBIE DUNCAN
illustrated by NINA OLLIKAINEN, MD

Rayve Productions Inc.

Rayve Productions Inc.
Box 726  Windsor CA 95492 USA

Printed in USA.

Publisher's Cataloging in Publication:
       Duncan,  Debbie.
     When Molly was in the hospital: a book for
brothers and sisters of hospitalized children / Debbie Duncan;
Nina Ollikainen, illustrator.
     p. cm. -- (MiniMed series)
     ISBN 1-877810-44-4
     SUMMARY:  Anna's little sister Molly needs to go to the
hospital for an operation.  In this sensitive and emotional story,
Anna tells about the experience from her point of view.


     1. Hospitals--Juvenile fiction. 2. Brothers and sisters--
Juvenile fiction. 3. Hospitals--Fiction. 4. Brothers and sisters--
Fiction.   I. Ollikainen, Nina, ill.  II. Title.


PZ7.D863When 1994                [E]

Library of Congress Catalog Number 94-67525

## Acknowledgments

This book would not have been possible without the assistance, cooperation, and encouragement from many individuals and institutions.  Debbie and Nina especially want to thank the Heck family — Cathy, Chris, Ana, Madeline, Emily, and Grandma Lee; the faculty, staff, and volunteers at Lucile Salter Packard Children's Hospital at Stanford and Stanford University Hospital; Deanna Hodgin; Marybeth Fox, MD; the "original" Grandma and Grandpa, Lavon and Don Duncan; Grandpa Al and Grandma Bea; our publishers, Barbara and Norm Ray; SuAnn and Kevin Kiser, Rita Seymour, and the other members of Debbie's writers group; Rebecca Gettelman; and our children's teachers and childcare providers, who gave us the time we needed to write and illustrate this story.

For Jennifer, Allison, Molly, and, of course, William.
— D.D.

To Ari, Alia, Mia, Noah, and Kaija with love.
— N.O.

I remember when my sister, Molly, was in the hospital.

Things in our house were a lot better before Molly got
sick. She used to like to play. Whenever I rolled a ball to her,
she said, "Thanks, Nanny."

My real name is Anna, but I love being "Nanny" to my baby sister.

One day Molly stopped playing with me. She stopped walking and eating too. All she wanted to do was sit in Mom's lap.

When I brought her a ball and one of her favorite books, she pushed them away. "No!" she cried. Molly wouldn't even look at me. That made me feel sad.

"Mom, can *you* play with me?" I asked.

Mom tried to put Molly down, but Molly screamed and Mom had to pick her up again.

I was so mad that for a minute I felt like being mean to Molly.

After a while, Mom and Molly spent more time at the doctor's office than they did at home. Dad said Molly needed lots of tests. "Are they like spelling tests?" I asked.

"No," Dad said, smiling a little. "They are x-rays and blood tests, and things like that."

When Mom was gone, Grandma and Grandpa sometimes came to stay with me after school. Sometimes I went to a friend's house. I like my friend's house, but I like my own house better.

One day Mom came home and said Molly needed to go
to the hospital to have an operation.  "Will that make her
better?" I asked.

Mom smiled.  "Yes.  We hope so."

"Will Molly have to stay in the hospital?"

"Dr. Amy thinks she'll have to stay for about a week."

"A week?  Why?"

"Because her body will need time to recover from surgery.
At the hospital there will be many people helping her get well
so she can come home again."

I got to go to the hospital the next day when Molly had her operation. Dad and Grandma and Grandpa and I sat in a waiting room across the hall while Mom talked to the doctors. The doctors all wore green suits that looked like pajamas, and had stethoscopes around their necks.

Mom held Molly until one of the doctors took her into
the operating room. Then a nurse gave Mom a beeper — just like
all the doctors at the hospital wear — so she could find Mom
as soon as the operation was over. Dad and Grandma and
Grandpa stayed in the waiting room, but Mom and I felt like
taking a walk.

It had been a long time since I had been alone with Mom.
First we went to the gift shop. I got to pick out a stuffed
animal for Molly and a book for me.

I held Mom's hand while we
walked up and down the halls of the
hospital. I tried to count the squares on
the floor, but mostly I tried not to step on a crack.
"I don't want to break your back and make *you*
have an operation," I told Mom.
"You're a goof," Mom said, squeezing my hand.
"And you know how much I love goofs."

After we threw pennies in the fountain outdoors, Mom
asked me if I wanted some lunch. We went to the cafeteria
and picked out our sandwiches, but as soon as we put our
trays on the table, Mom's beeper started beeping!

*Beep! Beep! Beep!*

"Grab your lunch," Mom said. "Let's hurry."

A doctor was talking to Dad and Grandma and Grandpa
when we got back to the waiting room. She said the surgery
had gone fine. She told us we were very lucky they could help
Molly.

A nurse pushed Molly in her big metal crib down the hall
to her room. Molly's room at the hospital was huge — much
bigger than the one we share at home.

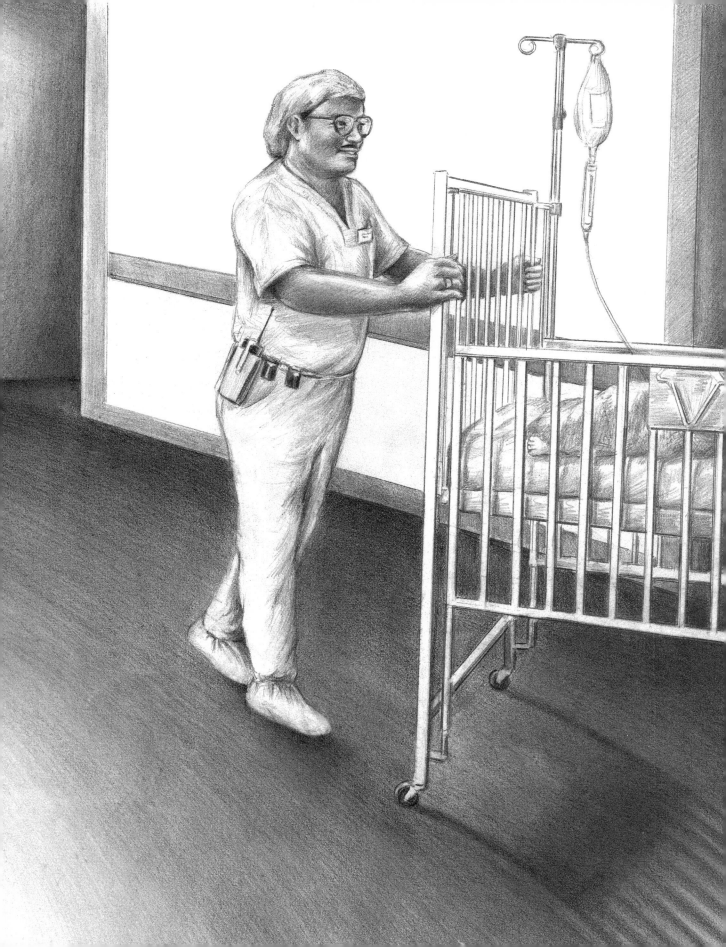

After the operation, Molly had tubes in her nose and her
arm, and a big bandage on her tummy.  I thought she looked
even sicker, and I was scared that she wouldn't get better.

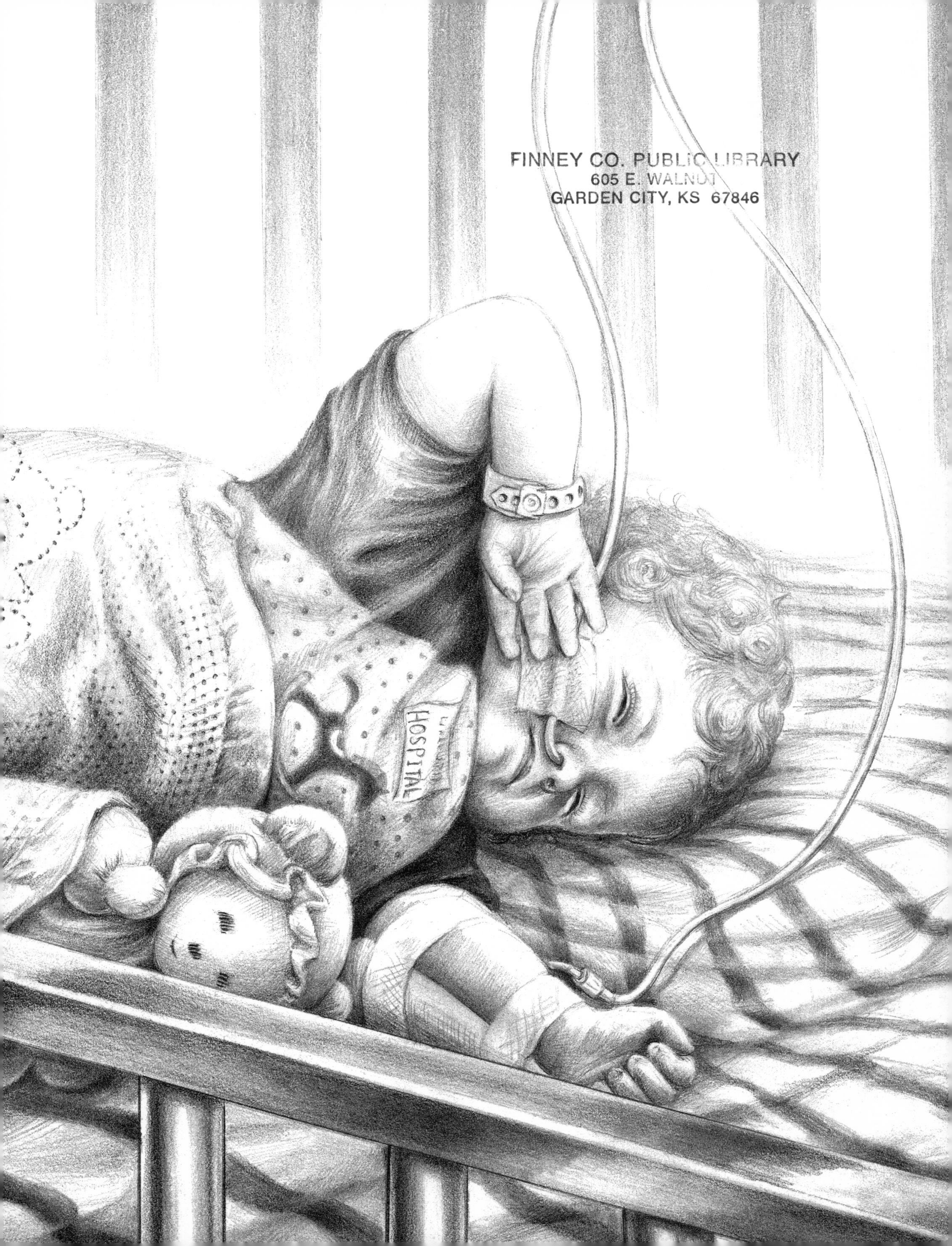
HOSPITAL

Mom and Dad took turns staying with Molly all night. I missed my mom when she wasn't home to tuck me in. I missed my sister when she wasn't there when I woke up in the morning.

I dreamed about Molly the night after her operation, and in my dream I pushed her off a chair. When I woke up, I was worried that I had been the one to make Molly sick. I felt awful.

I told Dad I was too tired to go to school, and he called Grandma to come stay with me. Pretty soon my ear started to hurt. Grandma took my temperature. "Merciful heavens!" she cried. "You have quite a fever."

Then I told Grandma about my scary dream. She said, "Anna, you had absolutely nothing to do with Molly's illness. It just happened. But I do need to take you to the doctor about your earache and fever."

"Will I have to have an operation like Molly?" I asked
Dr. Amy.

"No," she said. "You have an ear infection. You just need
some pink medicine."

I like Dr. Amy. I'm glad she's *my* doctor too.

Mom wouldn't let me visit the hospital until my fever went away. When I saw Molly again, she didn't quite smile, but she didn't look away either.

"Would you like to go with Molly to physical therapy?" Mom asked.

"What's that?"

"It's the work Molly has started doing here at the hospital, to learn how to walk and play again."

The physical therapy room was great! They had toys and balls and bikes and bars and ramps. I liked it a lot more than Molly did. She cried when she had to walk. The therapist said that's because Molly's muscles were sore from not being used for so long. I could see why Mom called it work.

When Molly was in the hospital, we ate dinner in the cafeteria instead of at home. I liked the french fries and chocolate milk.

Sometimes there were art projects for sisters and brothers. I made a sign that said MOLLY'S ROOM for her door, and a ceramic tile for the front of the hospital. But the best thing I made was a button for myself with my picture on it. Dad pinned it on my shirt.

On Saturday I spent the whole day at the hospital.  It was our best day.  I got to bring a ball back to Molly's room from physical therapy.  I rolled it to her . . . and she rolled it back to me! Mom and Dad and I cheered so loudly that we scared her and she cried.

"Easy does it," Mom said.  The next time we just smiled when she started playing with me, and Molly smiled too.

Then Dr. Amy came in with great news.  "I think Molly will be ready to go home on Monday."

"Wonderful!" Mom and Dad said together.

"Does that mean you'll tuck me in every night?" I asked Mom.

"Every night," said Mom.

I was so excited to see Molly when I got home from school on Monday. She even walked out to the play house. "I guess she wants some fresh air after all that time in the hospital," I said.

Mom gave me a hug.  She sure looked happy.

When Molly got well, Mom had time to play with me again.  I really liked that.  I asked Mom if we could take Molly to my class at school.  "I want to show everyone what her scar looks like."

"Sure," Mom said.  "But let's wait a couple of weeks to make sure she's well enough."

So Molly was my show-and-tell, and everyone asked lots of questions about the hospital and her operation.  I knew all the answers.  Sometimes I even felt like a doctor or a nurse. Mom brought Popsicles (Molly's favorite snack) for my whole class, and I got to pass them out.  I saved an orange one for Molly.  When I handed it to her, she looked at me and said, "Thanks, Nanny."

I love being "Nanny" to my sister.

## Author's Note

This story is based on our family's experience. When our daughter Molly was one, she had two operations before and after being diagnosed with celiac disease, a chronic illness caused by an intolerance for wheat, oats, barley, and rye. She has recovered fully and lives well on her gluten-free diet.

When a child is seriously ill and hospitalized, any other children in the family inevitably are affected. Molly's older sisters, Jennifer and Allison, experienced feelings of anger, loneliness, sadness, guilt, and worry while my husband and I tended to Molly's immediate needs. They also, however, learned about a new world called "the hospital," and felt real pride and joy during their sister's recovery. Their experience is shared every year by thousands of brothers and sisters of hospitalized children.

## About the Author

Debbie Duncan has published more than 50 essays in local and national newspapers and magazines. This is her first children's book. She graduated with honors in Humanities from Stanford University, and lives on the Stanford campus with her husband and their three daughters.

## About the Illustrator

Nina Ollikainen received a BS from Stanford University and an MD from the University of Southern California School of Medicine. After a long journey training to be a doctor, but seeing the world as an artist, Dr. Ollikainen changed direction and now devotes much of her time to writing and illustrating children's books. She limits her medical practice to teaching children the art of medicine and biology. Nina Ollikainen lives in Northern California with her husband and their four children, three cats, two rabbits, and one mouse.

# OTHER CHILDREN'S BOOKS & TAPES
# BY
# RAYVE PRODUCTIONS

## CHILDREN'S MULTICULTURAL BOOKS — TOUCAN TALES SERIES

Entertaining and educational children's books featuring intriguing folktales with
exquisite watercolor paintings set in different cultures around the world

### Nekane, the Lamiña & the Bear
#### A tale of the Basque Pyrenees
*Toucan Tales Volume 1*

by Frank P. Araujo, PhD ■ illustrations by Xiao Jun Li
ISBN 1-877810-01-0 ■ LC# 93-84620 ■ 10½x9 ■ Hardcover ■ 32 pages ■ 1993 ■ $16.95
■ Full color ■ In English with pronunciation guide and glossary for Basque words

### The Perfect Orange
#### A tale from Ethiopia
*Toucan Tales Volume 2*

by Frank P. Araujo, PhD ■ illustrations by Xiao Jun Li
ISBN 1-877810-94-0 ■ LC# 94-67524 ■ 10½x9 ■ Hardcover ■ 32 pages ■ 1994 ■ $16.95
■ Full color ■ In English with pronunciation guide and glossary for Ethiopian words

## OTHER CHILDREN'S BOOKS & TAPES

### The Laughing River
#### A folktale for peace

by Elizabeth Haze Vega ■ illustrations by Ashley Smith
ISBN 1-877810-35-5 ■ 10x8 ■ Hardcover ■ 32 pages ■ Fall 1994 ■ $16.95 ■ Full color
■ Includes story, written music and lyrics ■ Instructions for related dance and for
making and playing drum.

### The Laughing River audio cassette tape

by Elizabeth Haze Vega ■ accompaniment by Bobby Vega
Cassette $9.95 ■ Book and cassette tape combination $23.95

### Night Sounds

by Lois G. Grambling ■ illustrations by Randall F. Ray
ISBN 1-877810-77-0 ■ 8x10 ■ Hardcover ■ B/W graphite illustrations ■ 32 pages ■
Spring 1995 ■ $12.95 ■ What does a child hear when falling asleep? A variety of
sounds that stir the imagination and gently lull one to sleep.

RAYVE PRODUCTIONS INC ■ PO BOX 726 ■ WINDSOR CA 95492
PHONE 707.838.6200 ■ FAX 707.838.2220 ■ ORDER 800.852.4890